Nov. 2015

Published in 2016 by **Windmill Books**,
an Imprint of Rosen Publishing
29 East 21st Street, New York, NY 10010

Copyright © 2016 Blake Publishing

Photography: Dreamstime; Steve Parish/Nature-Connect:
p. 2; Narinda Sandry: pp. 3, 4, 5 (larvae), 6, 10, 13,
18, 23, IBC (pupa, eggs).
Photo research: Emma Harm
Cover and text design: Leanne Nobilio
Color management: Greg Harm
Editor: Vanessa Barker

Library of Congress Cataloging-in-Publication Data

Johnson, Rebecca.
Mia the mosquito's book of dirty tricks /
by Rebecca Johnson.
p. cm. — (Bug Adventures)
Includes index.
ISBN 978-1-4777-5617-1 (pbk.)
ISBN 978-1-4777-5616-4 (6 pack)
ISBN 978-1-4777-5540-2 (library binding)
1. Mosquitoes — Juvenile literature.
I. Johnson, Rebecca, 1966-. II. Title.
QL536.J683 2016
595.77—d23

Manufactured in the United States of America
CPSIA Compliance Information: Batch WS15WM; For Further Information
contact Rosen Publishing, New York, New York at 1-800-237-9932

BUG ADVENTURES

CONTENTS

Great spot!

Trick 1

Find some water to lay your eggs. Make sure it is water that won't get tipped over every week.

2

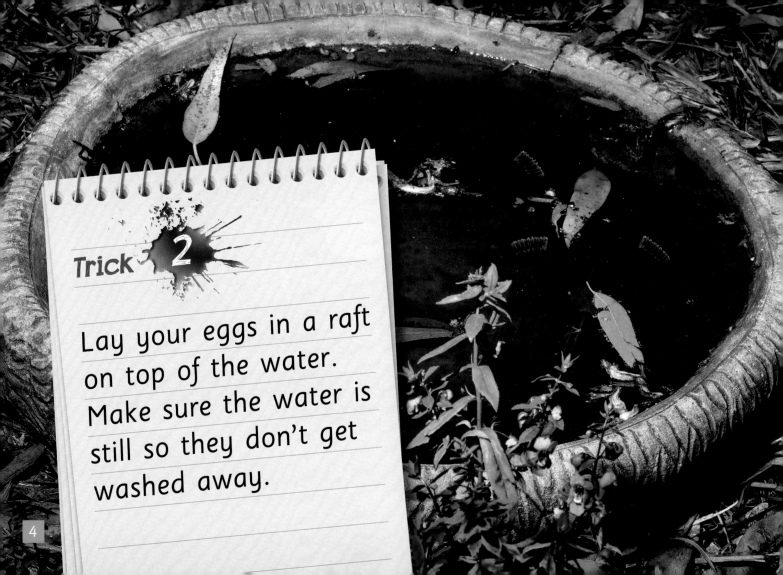

Trick 2

Lay your eggs in a raft on top of the water. Make sure the water is still so they don't get washed away.

Trick 3

Wigglers, when you hatch, try to look as much like little sticks as you can. Wiggle like mad if something tries to eat you! Stay like this for seven to ten days.

Like sticks

Use the breathing tube that is located in your backside to breathe when you come to the surface. That way birds won't see you, but it doesn't mean you won't have bad breath!

Breathing tube

Pupa

Trick 5

You're going to molt four times. Don't worry! When this happens, it just means you're growing and getting bigger. On the fourth molt, you'll turn into a pupa.

Trick 6

Make sure you eat loads of food before you become a pupa. Fill up on lots of tiny animals and plants, because you won't be able to eat in this stage.

Dinner

Trick 7

The good news is you're only going to be a pupa for two days. This stage is going to be scary for you. Lots of fish and other things will try to eat you.

Watch out! ⟶

Siphons

Breathe through the siphons on your back and get ready for the last stage.

Time for takeoff! Soon your back is going to split open (ouch!) and you can fly out of the old pupa.

11

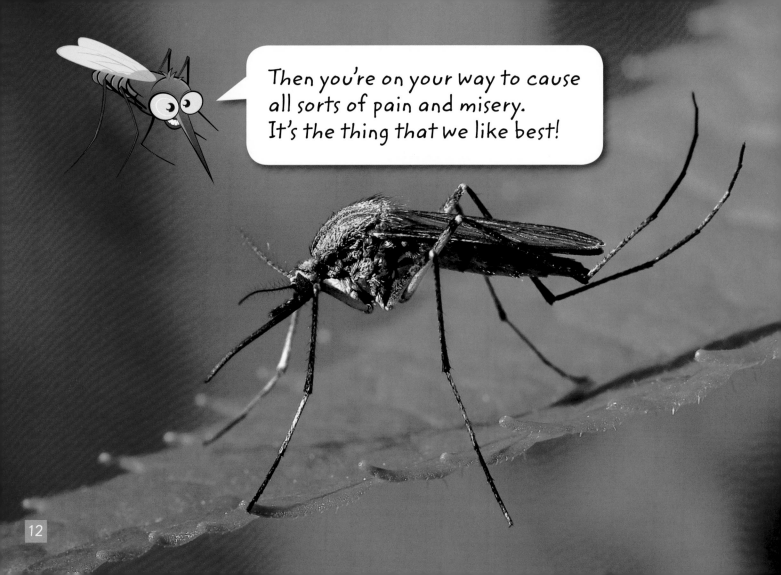

Trick 9

Boys, you've got the easy job. You just need to find nectar and plant juices and mate with the girls.

Sweet treat

Bite hard!

You'll know which ones are the girls. They are the only ones that can buzz and make all the noise.

Poison

Trick 10

Girls, you've got the tough job. You have to find blood to feed the eggs inside you. Animals or humans will do, and this can be tricky as they have all sorts of ways to get you.

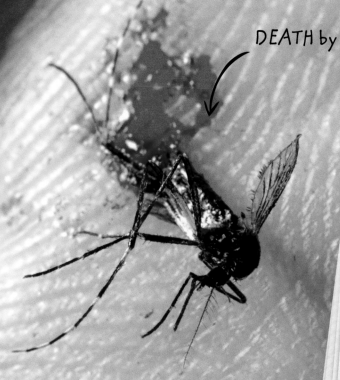

DEATH by the SLAP!

Trick **11**

Watch out for fly sprays, mosquito coils, and (worst of all) the slap, or it could all be over pretty quickly.

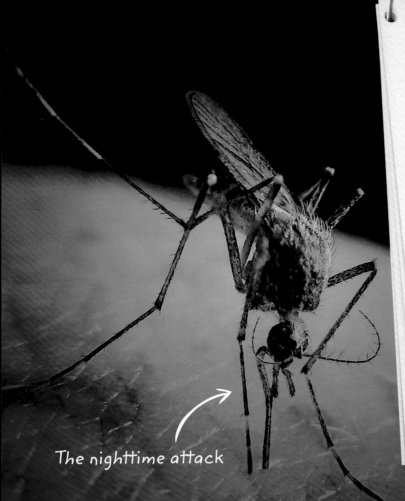

The nighttime attack

Trick 12

Do your thing in the dark. This is the smartest way to go. You can smell blood from 100 feet away, and in the dark is the best way to sneak up on your victims.

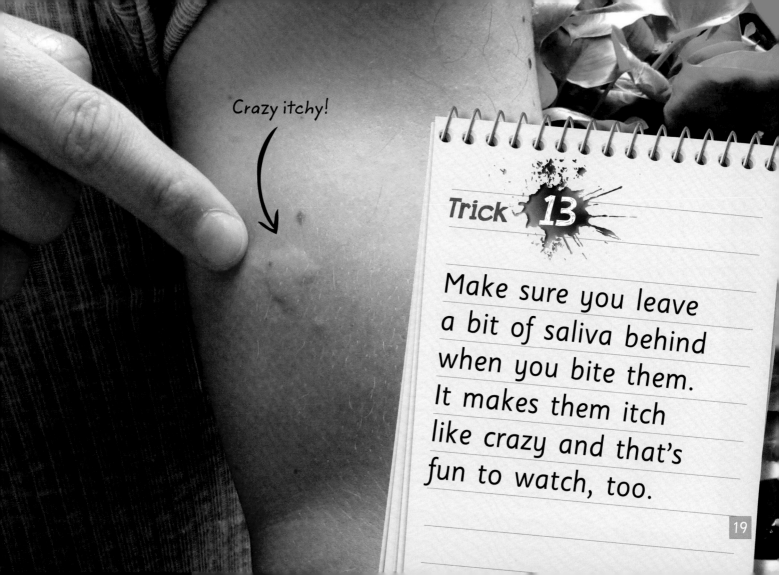

Crazy itchy!

Trick 13

Make sure you leave a bit of saliva behind when you bite them. It makes them itch like crazy and that's fun to watch, too.

19

Trick 14

Last but not least, don't forget to pack those diseases. If you can, try to carry malaria, yellow fever, or dengue fever, as they are my personal favorites.

MALARIA

YELLOW FEVER

DENGUE FEVER

Fill up on blood

One good bite and your victims are in real trouble.

21

Okay mosquitoes, you know what to do. We're gaining forces and we now have over 2,500 different species around the world.

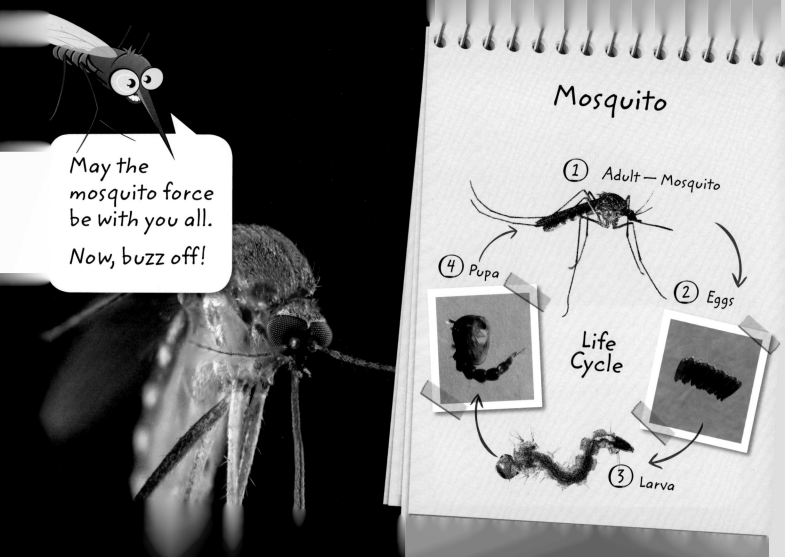